'Well,' said Eppie, 'ev
desperately want to be
gap between Mum's te
agree to your demands.'

'Then you're just going to have to stay
there for ever while I crawl over to the
edge of Mum's mouth and jump out to
freedom.'

'All right, Zeke,' said Eppie calmly.
'Good luck when you jump. Oh and
especially good luck when you explain to
Mum just where I am and how I got here
in the first place. Will you tell her how
you shrank me and took me to school in
your pocket, or just the bit about sending
me off into space with your stupid yo-yo
trick, or maybe you'll just tell her how
you put too many bubbles in the bath and I
slipped down the plughole and under the sea
where a man-o'-war-stinging-thing
tried to kill me!!!!!!!!!!!'

'Uh oh,' said Zeke. 'I forgot about all
that.'

My Sister's a

Burp

MY SISTER'S A BURP
A RED FOX BOOK 0 09 944808 4

Published in Great Britain by Red Fox,
an imprint of Random House Children's Books

PRINTING HISTORY
First published in Australia by Random House Australia Pty Ltd, 1999
Red Fox edition published, 2003

1 3 5 7 9 10 8 6 4 2

Red Fox books are published by Random House Children's Books,
61–63 Uxbridge Road, London W5 5SA,
a division of The Random House Group Ltd,
in Australia by Random House Australia (Pty) Ltd,
20 Alfred Street, Milsons Point, Sydney, NSW 2061, Australia,
in New Zealand by Random House New Zealand Ltd,
18 Poland Road, Glenfield, Auckland 10, New Zealand,
and in South Africa by Random House (Pty) Ltd,
Endulini, 5A Jubilee Road, Parktown 2193, South Africa

THE RANDOM HOUSE GROUP Limited Reg. No. 954009

A CIP catalogue record for this book is available from the British Library.

Printed and bound in Great Britain by Cox & Wyman Ltd, Reading, Berkshire

www.kidsatrandomhouse.co.uk

GRETEL KILLEEN

My Sister's a

Burp

Illustrated by Zeke and Eppie

RED FOX

A message from your author...

A big 'Gooday' from the top (or the bottom) of the world, depending on which way you look at it. An Aussie life is very different to a Pommie life. It's very hot, pretty dry and we have bugs, spiders and sea life that can kill you. But we also have fabulous creatures that won't hurt and might try to kiss you (if you've brushed your hair and are looking quite attractive). In this adventure you'll read about a **kookaburra** (which is a meat-eating bird that sits up in trees and laughs), a **wombat** (which is a short-legged, slow-moving rectangle of fur with a face like a bear) and a **platypus** (which is an ancient weird-looking creature that some say possesses magical powers and others say is just an ancient weird-looking creature).

Now start reading before we all come along and try to eat you
(only joking – we're on a diet).

It's not every day that your mother **swallows** you. Because it's not every day that your sister shrinks to the size of a strawberry, gets a yo-yo tangled in her hair and then ends up in outer space where she has to be rescued from Planet Sock by you and the man in the moon. And it's not every day that you and your sister return from space riding on a meteor and the amazing speed stretches you both very long and thin like pieces of spaghetti so that when you finally do get home you get sucked down the bathroom plughole. Oh no, it's not every day that you end up in the pipes and drains under your house, get zapped by an electric eel, shrunk again to the size of a ladybird, snuggled by a shark (who's pretending to be seaweed), rescued by a merprincess, attacked by soldier crabs and disguised as sea slugs. And it's not every day that you get stranded on a desert island, evaporated like water droplets, and delivered by the stork to your very own back garden where your mother promptly swallows you!!!! But that's what had happened so far today.

Zeke and Eppie were caught in their mum's throat.

Cough, cough, cough, went Mum as she tried to clear the tickle in her throat.

'H E L P!' yelled little Eppie as she tried to stop herself tumbling down her mum's oesophagus and into her grizzly gizzards.

'H
E
L
P!' roared Zeke when
Eppie tried to grab onto him. 'What are
you trying to do? As if being swallowed
by your mum isn't enough, now you're
trying to kill me by hugging me and
giving me your disgusting girls' germs.'

'I'm not trying to kill you,' said Eppie.
'And I'm certainly not trying to hug
you. I accidentally grabbed onto your
waist because I thought you were one
of Mum's tonsils.'

'WHAT!' bellowed Zeke in frustration
as he managed to crawl safely out of
his mum's throat and land **thump** on
the moon-like surface of his mother's

tongue. 'How could you possibly think I look like a tonsil?'

'Everyone thinks you look like a tonsil, Zeke,' said Eppie as she landed splat beside him. 'Because you're a long pink slimy blob.'

'What on earth is wrong with you?' Zeke yelled as he tried not to go pink with rage like a tonsil with tonsillitis. 'Have aliens stolen your brain? Have they emptied your head and filled it up with pairs of Grandma's underpants? Have your head and your bottom been swapped around? Everyone doesn't say I look like a tonsil. They say I look like Tom Cruise.'

'Tonsil,' said Eppie.

'Tom Cruise,' said Zeke.

'Tonsil,' said Eppie.

'Tom Cruise,' said Zeke.

'Tonsil.'

'Tom Cruise.'

'Tonsil Cruise.'

'Tom Cruise,' thundered Zeke as he went to pull his sister's hair. Eppie was just about to say something really brilliant but before she could get her extraordinary words out of her mini mouth she was very rudely interrupted by the sort of great trembling squishy sound that everybody knows can only be made by an approaching wave of spit.

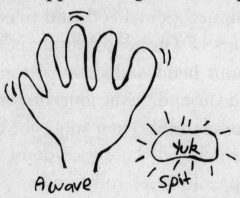

A wave

Spit

Yuk

'Oh no, Mum's trying to wash us down with spit! If we don't grab onto something fast we're going to get flushed down into her gizzards!' said Eppie.

'Oh gross,' said Zeke as he saw the

waves of spit come rolling fast and close, 'I wish I had my boogie board here.'

'I wish you did too,' said Eppie. 'Then you could rescue me.'

'Actually,' said Zeke, 'I *can* rescue you, if you pretend to be my boogie board.'

'What!' said Eppie with a look on her little face like she'd just seen a stinking dead rat.

'Yeah,' said Zeke. 'You lie flat and I'll ride us out of here.'

The spit was coming like a marching army rolling steadily towards them. 'I'm not pretending to be your boogie board!' said Eppie. 'I would rather wear a pair of boy's undies on my head and sing *tiddly winks tiddly winks oh lacky lay* while I danced like a hulaladyeeeeeeeeeeeeee eeeeeeeeeeeeeeeeeeeeeeeeeeeeee eeeeeeeeeeeeeeeeeeeeeeeeeeeeee

eeeeeeeeeeeeeeeeeeeeeeeeeeeeeeeeeeee
eeeeeeeeeeeeeeeeeeeeeeeeeeeeeeeeeeeee
eeeeee!'

And with that Zeke and Eppie were swept off Mum's tongue and caught in a strong current of gooey soppy spittle.

'Aaaaaaaaaaaaaaaa aaaaaaaaaaaaaaaaaaa aaaaaaaaaaaaaaagh!'

roared Eppie and Zeke together.

'Oh no, we're goners,' they whimpered.

They held hands, but don't tell anybody, and together Zeke and Eppie were rumbled and tumbled just like in surf and they definitely would have gone straight down to Mum's tummy if it weren't for the very simple fact that in all of that whirling and gefurdling about Eppie got stuck between two of Mum's teeth. And because Zeke was holding onto his sister's hand (oh gross!) he didn't get washed down his mum's throat either.

'So Zeke,' said Eppie as she lay squished between two of her mother's back molars, 'looks to me like I've saved your life. Boy do you owe me a favour! I think that you should promise right here and now that you will make my bed every morning and give me official power over the TV remote control.'

'Actually Eppie,' Zeke replied as he let go of Eppie's hand and tried to wipe her germs off on his shorts, 'it seems to me that you need my help now. So if you want me to save your life I suggest you start promising that you will not only make my bed every morning, and give me official power over the remote control, but you will also let me sit in the front seat every time Mum drives us anywhere . . . and that you'll eat all the vegetables and burnt things that Mum gives us for dinner.'

'Burnt things! But that includes nearly all Mum's cooking!' gasped Eppie. 'It sounds like a terrible deal. Does it include brussels sprouts?'

'Yes, it does include brussels sprouts,' replied Zeke.

'Well,' said Eppie, 'even though I desperately want to be removed from this gap between Mum's teeth I cannot possibly agree to your demands.'

'Then you're just going to have to stay there for ever while I crawl over to the edge of Mum's mouth and jump out to freedom.'

'All right, Zeke,' said Eppie calmly. 'Good luck when you jump. Oh and especially good luck when you explain to Mum just where I am and how I got here in the first place. Will you tell her how you shrank me and took me to school in your pocket, or just the bit about sending me off into space with your stupid yo-yo trick, or maybe you'll just tell her how you put too many bubbles in the bath and I slipped down the plughole and under the sea where a man-o'-war-stinging-thing tried to

Kill me!!!!!!!!!!!!!!!!! !!!!!!!!!!!!!!!!!!!!!!'

'Uh oh,' said Zeke. 'I forgot about all that.'

'Yes, smarty pants, so now what are we going to do?' said Eppie.

'Well I guess I'll just have to try to pull you out,' sighed Zeke. And with that Zeke blocked his nose with one hand and grabbed onto Eppie's foot with the other.

'Breathe in when I say "*now*",' said Zeke.

'Now?' said Eppie.

'No, when I say "one, two, three, *now*",' said Zeke.

'Now?' teased Eppie.

'Stop bugging me Eppie,' Zeke replied, 'or I'll escape from here and live with monkeys in the jungle for the rest of my life and never tell Mum anything.'

'OK,' said Eppie.

'One, two, three, *now*,' yelled Zeke and he pulled as hard as he could and Eppie breathed in. But absolutely nothing happened.

monkey   zeke

'Why don't you use two hands, you flea brain?' said Eppie.

'Because I have to block my nose with one hand so I don't smell your stinking feet,' said Zeke.

'My feet don't smell,' said Eppie.

'Oh yes they do!'

'Oh no they don't,' said Eppie.

'Oh yes they do,' said the chewing gums.

'Oh no they don't,' said the two front teeth.

'Oh for heaven's sake,' interrupted a gold filling snootily. 'If you really want to know if they stink or not why don't you ask the wisdom teeth?'

'OK,' said the cheeks cheekily.

And so the wisdom teeth held a quick meeting to decide if Eppie's feet stank or not. Each wise tooth stopped to sniff the air, and then they all announced their decision.

'We have decided,' said the head wisdom tooth, 'after carefully studying this issue, that Eppie's feet do *not* smell, but something does and it is possibly Zeke.'

'Yeah, ha ha ha ha ha ha ha,' said Eppie.

'Oh bum,' said Zeke.

'No, feet,' said the fillings, giggling ridiculously until all the teeth joined in.

'I'm sorry,' said a back molar. 'You must forgive the teeth for guffawing.

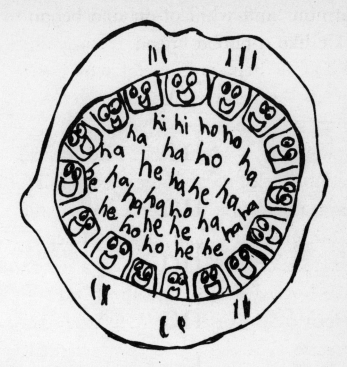

You see we went to the dentist only this morning and he gave us so much laughing gas that I'm afraid it hasn't quite worn off.'

'Well maybe it's the gas that smells so bad,' said Zeke, 'because I smell like a bunch of roses.'

'What gas?' said Eppie. 'I don't smell a thing.' And with that she took an enormous sniff-whiff of air and began to cackle like a bubba hyena.

'A
ha
ha
ha
ha
ha,'

laughed Eppie. But Zeke didn't get the joke.

'You should stop laughing, Eppie,' said Zeke, 'because all this giggle-jiggling will annoy Mum. And besides, I know you're only pretending to laugh because your face suddenly looks like a pig and whenever you're pretending anything at

all you always look like a pig. Your
face gets all squishy and your nose goes
all flat and you make a sort of snorting
sound exactly like a pig.'

Then Zeke pretended to be Eppie
pretending to be a pig and began to
breathe very loudly through the back of
his mouth and snort and snort and
snort. And lo and behold if he didn't
find himself inhaling the happy gas too
and laughing along with the sniggling
teeth and the fun-filled fillings.

'A
ha
ha
ha
ha
ha!!!!!!!!!!!!!!!'

Louder and louder and louder they laughed like drunken kookaburras. They laughed so hard they were sure their mother would hear. But, of course, she didn't hear a thing from her tiny little children ha ha-ing in her mouth. But she did *feel* something she didn't quite like and that was a jiggling wiggling giggling thing stuck between her teeth.

'What on earth is that?' wondered Zeke and Eppie's mother as she swooped her tongue in Eppie's direction and knocked Zeke, fling smash, into the inside of her cheek.

Splat!

'Watch out!' yelled Zeke to Eppie while she tried to squirm away from the attacking tongue. But before you could say 'hawupwupwup', Eppie was being picked and pushed by her mother's tongue like a puppy slobbering all over your face.

'Get me out of here!' screamed Eppie.

'Just stay still,' Zeke called as he finished sort of rock climbing to the top of Mum's mouth and dangled from Mum's top row of teeth. 'Just stay absolutely still and Mum will think you've gone away.'

So Eppie lay as still as she could and sure enough after a short while the tongue stopped attacking her.

'Phew,' sighed Eppie. 'That was close.'

'Look out!'

yelled Zeke.

But it was too late because Eppie was suddenly attacked, right then and there, by an enormous hand carrying a small wooden spear.

'Look out!' yelled the teeth. 'She's got a toothpick!' You could hear the teeth chattering 'not me, not me, not me' but the toothpick didn't go anywhere near them and went straight for Eppie instead.

'Defend yourself,' called the teeth.

'Help,' screamed Eppie as the wooden sword came poking close. 'Help me, Zeke!' Eppie screamed as she looked up to see that Zeke was still clinging to the row of teeth above her and apparently doing absolutely nothing.

'What?' yelled Zeke.

'I said *Help me Zeke*,' said Eppie.

'Help me Zeke what?' said Zeke.

'Help me Zeke PLEASE,' pleaded Eppie angrily as the toothpick came frighteningly close.

'Help me Zeke please and I promise that I will be your slave for the rest of my life and what else?' said Zeke.

'I'll tell you what else!'

boomed Mum's sharp incisor tooth. 'You get down and rescue your little sister or I'm going to chew you to smithereens and then spit you out into an ant hill.'

'Boy,' said Zeke. 'That's a bit harsh. I was only trying to negotiate a deal. No wonder you are only teeth stuck in a greasy grimy gob for your entire lives.'

'What did you say?' roared the teeth together.

'I said it's obvious you don't have a sister and haven't got a clue about anything at all because of course I was going to help Eppie. I was just teasing her first like brothers are supposed to.'

'Get him!!!!!!!!!!!!!!!!!!!!' yelled the molars.

'Yeah get him!' they all squealed. And just as Zeke managed to duck behind a molar the teeth began to grind angrily.

'Um, excuse me,' said Eppie, 'I hate to interrupt this ridiculous fight but may I just remind you that the person this fight is all about, ME, has just fought and won a battle with a newly broken toothpick and is feeling very weak,' spluttered Eppie.

'Don't worry, I'll rescue you,' yelled Zeke just like a really handsome hero who was the size of a blowfly and hiding behind a tooth.

'I will come and save your life!' he sang as he hurled himself with a leapfrog from tooth to tooth and landed splat thwack on Eppie.

'Good aim,' groaned Eppie under Zeke's weight. 'Now, get me out of here!'

Zeke squiggled and squirmed for a couple of seconds and then said, 'I'm afraid I can't.'

'What do you mean you can't!' said Eppie. 'Don't you remember what our mum always says?'

'No,' said Zeke.

'No, me either,' said Eppie. 'But I know it was important.'

'Well I want to get off you Eppie because as you know I think you smell like chicken droppings, but unfortunately the position I'm in means I simply can't get off.'

So Zeke and Eppie tried wiggling together but only managed to burrow themselves further down the gap between Mum's teeth.

'I can't believe the toothpick broke!' said Mum as she rummaged through the kitchen drawers looking for something else to fix her itchy teeth. 'Whatever it is that's stuck between my teeth is really driving me insane.' And with that Mum headed upstairs to the bathroom to find her dental floss.

'She's going up to the bathroom to find her dental floss!' said the eyes to the nose who told the mouth who told the teeth who told tiny little Zeke and Eppie.

'Oh no,' said Zeke, 'one wrong move from that piece of sharp floss and we could end up losing our heads!'

'We're opening the bathroom cabinet,' said the fingers.

'I know, I can hear you,' said the ears.

'We're pretending we can't see the dental floss,' said the eyes.

'I sense Brain will find some other sneaky way to find the floss,' said the feelings.

'But why would Brain betray her own body?' gasped Eppie in shock.

'Because Brain is a crawler and does absolutely anything to try and make your mum happy,' said the tummy button.

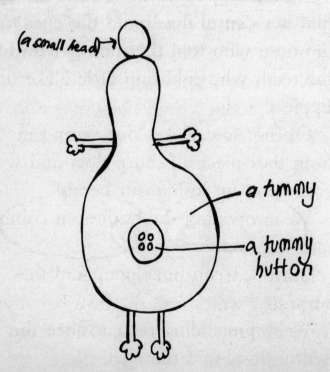

(a small head →

a tummy

a tummy button

'We must stop Brain finding the dental floss or these tiny weeny smaller than sultana children will definitely lose their heads!' said snot, who looked sort of awful but was actually a really, really nice guy.

'Right Hand, close the bathroom cabinet door,' said the tongue urgently.

'I can't, Brain won't let me,' waved the hand.

'Well what about you Left Hand? Can you close the door?' asked Tonsil.

'No, I can't,' sighed the left hand disappointedly. 'Brain has put me in Mum's pocket while he makes Eyes look for the floss.'

'Don't worry,' said the eyes. 'We purposely won't find the floss because we're making ourselves go all blurry and we're both looking at Nose.'

'Good,' said the wisdom teeth, 'that will give us a moment to gather our thoughts and work out how to protect midget Zeke and Eppie.'

'Oh this is so sad,' sobbed the heart.

'For heaven's sake Heart,' teased the hair, 'could you stop your whimpering and think of a solution?'

'All right,' said the heart. 'I'll be brave.'

'Well you'd better hurry up,' said the left elbow, 'because Brain's going through her memory bank photo album to try and find a shot with the floss in it.

 That way she'll know exactly where the floss is in the cupboard and she'll find it without Eyes' help.'

'She's found the floss!' screamed the thumb.

'She's reaching for it,' pouted the lips.

'Quick Zeke and Eppie,' said the heart soothingly. 'Give each other a cuddle.'

'Give each other a cuddle!' blurted the bottom. 'What use is that going to be?'

'Well,' said the heart very patiently to the bottom, 'it will make them feel safe and secure in this moment of terror.'

'What!' bellowed Bottom. 'What is the point in **feeeeeeeeeeeeeeeeeeeeeeeeeeeling** safe and secure when your head is about to be cut off?'

'I agree completely,' said Zeke, 'and what's more, if I am about to die I certainly don't want to be found lying here hugging my sister. In fact the mere thought of being found dead like that would absolutely kill me!'

'The floss is coming, the floss is coming!' cried the freckles on Mum's nose.

But there was nothing Zeke and Eppie could do.

37

They couldn't run, they couldn't hide, they couldn't even roll into a ball. All they could do was gently lie squished together between Mum's teeth and say their fond farewells.

'Bye Zeke,' said Eppie, trying not to cry. 'I don't really think you're a boy's bra.'

'Bye Eppie,' said Zeke. 'You don't really look like a pig's bum.' Then they blew raspberry kisses to each other,

'Bpppppthththththtth'
'Bpppppppthththtth,'

and waited for their heads to be chopped off.

'WAIT!' screeched the gooey

wax that lives in people's ears. 'I have had a brilliant idea!'

'What?' chortled the chin.

'Shut your mouth,' said the ear wax.

'I beg your pardon?' gasped the lungs.

'I said, "shut your mouth!"' said the wax as he started to get all hot and bothered and go a little runny.

'How rude and revolting,' said the shoulders.

'Well, what do you expect from Ear Wax?' said the knees. 'He's positively disgusting.'

'Shut your mouth!' said the hot and flustered wax once more before he dribbled out the ear and onto the floor.

'Gross!' said everyone all together. 'What on earth could Ear Wax mean?'

'Oh I get it, ha ha!' laughed the funny bone. 'Wax means *shut your mouth* because if the mouth is shut then the floss can't get in!'

'Oh,' said everyone together. And so Mouth quickly shut herself tight so Mum couldn't get the dental floss in.

It was warm and dark inside Mum's mouth.

Mum's closed mouth

'Now what do we do?' said Eppie.

'We're just going to have to lie very still so that Mum forgets that she ever wanted to use floss at all and then Mouth can open up again,' said Zeke.

'Mum's not going to forget she ever needed floss,' insisted Eppie.

'Are you kidding?' replied Zeke. 'Our Mum could forget anything. Don't you remember when you were born and Mum left the hospital without you? Or what about the time she forgot where she'd put her glasses and spent a whole day with them on top of her head? Or what about when we go shopping and she loses the car because she forgets where she's parked it? And what about the time she went to leave for work wearing only her underwear because she'd forgotten to put her clothes on!'

'Oh yeah, you're right,' said Eppie. 'If we just sit tight and don't make a move Mum will definitely forget she wanted to floss.'

Dum de dum de dum

'Want to play I-spy?' whispered the tonsils.

'Not really,' said the teeth, the tongue, Eppie, Zeke and the roof of Mum's mouth.

'Oh please play I-spy,' said the tonsils.

'No,' said the teeth, the tongue, Eppie, Zeke and the roof of Mum's mouth.

'Oh pleeeeeeeeeeeeeeeeeeeeeeeeeeeeeeeee
eeeeeeeeeeeeeeeeeeeeeeeeeeeeeeeeeeeeeeee
eeeeeeeeeeeeeeeeeeeeeeeeeeeeeeeeeeeeeeee
eeeeeeeeeeeeeeeeeeeeeeeeeeeeeeeeeeeeeeee
eeeeeeeeeeeeeeeeeeeeeeeeeeeeeeeeeeeeeeee
eeeeeeeeeeeeeeeeeeeeeeeeeeeeeeeeeeeeeeee
eeeeeeeeeeeeeeeeeeeeeeeeeeeeeeeeeeeeeeee
eeeeeeeeeeeeeeeeeeeeeeeeeeeeeeeeeeeeeeee
eeeeeeeeeeeeeeeeeeeeeeeeeeeeeeeeeeeeeeee
eeeeeeeeeeeeeeeeeeeeeeeeeeeeeeeeeeeeeeee
eeeeeeeeeeeeeeeeeeeeeeeeeeeeeeeeeeeeeeee
eeeeeeeeeeeeeeeeeeeeeeeeeeeeeeeeeeeeeeee
eeeeeeeeeeeeeeeeeeeeeeeeeeeeeeeeeeeeeeee
eeeeeeeeeeeeeeeeeeeeeeeeeeeeeeeeeeeeeeee
eeeeeeeeeeeeeeeeeeeeeeeeeeeeeeeeeeeeeeee
eeeeeeeeeeeeeeeeeeeeeeeeeeeeeeeeeeeeeeee
eeeeeeeeeeeeeeeeeeeeeeeeeeeeeeeeeeeeeeee
eeeeeeeeeeeeeeeeeeeeeeeeeeeeeeeeeeeeeeee
eeeeeeeeeeeeeeeeeeeeeeeeeeeeeeeeeeeeeeee
eeeeeeeeeeeeeeeeeeeeeeeeeeeeeeeeeeeeeeee
eeeeeeeeeeeeeeeeeeeeeeeeeeeeeeeeeeeeeeee
eeeeeeeeeeeeeeeeease!' begged the tonsils.

'Oh all right,' said the teeth, the tongue, Eppie, Zeke and the roof of Mum's mouth.

'Cool,' said the tonsils. 'OK then, here we go. I spy with my little eye something beginning with D.'

'DARK!' chorused the teeth, the tongue, Eppie, Zeke and the roof of Mum's mouth.

'Boy,' said the disappointed tonsils. 'How did you guess that!'

happy tonsil   depressed tonsil

So Zeke and Eppie were safe in the shut mouth but just to make sure that Mum didn't try any other tricks, Mum's body decided that the mouth wouldn't open again for at least seventeen minutes and fourteen seconds, which should be long enough for Zeke and Eppie to escape. Of course Zeke and Eppie were getting a little hot and a little damp but at least they still had their heads. But what about Mum? Well, she also still had her head but about one minute ago she had suddenly found that she couldn't open her mouth.

'MMM! MMM!' said Mum, which is closed-mouth language for

'HELP! HELP!' And so Mum yelled and yelled and yelled but no one could hear her, let alone understand her, because dear old mum had her mouth shut tight. So Mum sat on the toilet, with the lid down of course, and wondered what to do. Her first thought was that someone had placed an evil spell on her; perhaps the neighbour's parrot who Mum was always telling to be quiet, or the lady at the corner shop who looked like a meringue and never gave anybody the right change *and* pretended she was deaf when anyone complained. Or perhaps the dribbly purple-haired man at the end of the road who chased Mum all the way down the street yesterday and then bit her on the ankle like a mad dog.

First off Mum went to the neighbour's house and asked, 'MMMMMMmmmmmm mm mm m mm m?'

'No of course I didn't put you under a magic spell,' the neighbour's parrot kindly replied. 'But why don't you try the meringue lady at the corner store, she's always putting secret spells on people she doesn't like.'

So the shut-mouth-mother of Zeke and Eppie went to the corner store.

'Mmmmm mmmm MMMMMMM mmmm mmmmmmm m?' she said.

'No,' replied the lady who looked like a meringue, 'I didn't put a magic spell on you. I couldn't possibly afford the ingredients the way everyone who comes here demands the right change. Why don't you try that horrible purple-haired man who thinks he's a dog?'

And so that's what Zeke and Eppie's mother did. 'Mmmm mmm mm mmmm mmm mm m mmm mmm?' she said to the man who chased cars and bit people's ankles.

'Woof woof,' he howled and then rolled onto his back like he wanted Mum to rub his tummy.

'Aaaaaaaaaaaaaaaaaaaaaaaaaaaaaaaaa aaaaaaaaaaaaaaaaaaaaaaaaaagh gross!' thought Mum to herself. 'That man is about as smart as a chop. He could never master a magic spell.'

So with no one left on her Who Put A Spell On Me? list, Zeke and Eppie's mother had absolutely no choice but to take herself off to the doctor to discover why her mouth wouldn't open.

'Oh dear,' Mum thought. 'This is getting urgent. I wish I had a siren to put on my car so that people would think I was an ambulance.'

And just then Mum spotted the cat and made a sort of 'a huh, you'll do' sound. Then Mum and the cat got in the car and the cat sat in the front seat with his head sticking out the window and he made a 'meow' noise that sounded just like a siren as they travelled all the way round the block to the doctor's surgery.

'Meeeeeeeeeeeeeeeeeeeeeeeeeeeeeeeeeeeow, Meeeeeeeeeeeeeeeeeeeeeeeeeeeeeeeeeeeow, Meeeeeeeeeeeeeeeeeeeeeeeeeeeow,' went the cat and all the traffic moved right out of their way (including a getaway van that was carrying three robbers who had just held up a bank while wearing elephant masks).

As soon as they arrived at the doctor's surgery the cat sat on the mat while Mum tried to explain to the receptionist just what was wrong. But it's hard to explain something when your mouth

won't open, so in desperation Mum
finally made a face like a cross-eyed fish
and pretended to faint on
the floor. And then the cat
sat on her head.

'Oi moy godness,' said the
receptionist while she sucked
on a huge boiled lolly.
'Oi'd bitter git tha docta!'

The cat waited for Mum
to be diagnosed and then
after about two minutes she said, 'I'm
bored, there's nothing to do here. I'm
going off to shop.' And so she took
Mum's credit card out of her bag and
went to the pet shop to find a fabulous
new cat suit.

cat suit   cat hood

Meanwhile, Mum was in the doctor's surgery getting sneezed on by the doctor.

'Hello Madam achoooooo,' said the doctor. 'Now what achooo seems achoo to be the achoo problem achooooooo hooooooooooo hoooooooooooooooooooo?'

Zeke and Eppie's mum wanted to explain that she couldn't open her mouth, but before she could even begin to explain she suddenly needed to sneeze. 'Oh no!' thought Mum. 'I've caught the doctor's cold! Oh no, oh no, oh no!'

Now normally catching a cold wouldn't really matter that much. You'd just get the sniffles and maybe an earache and perhaps a sore throat, and you'd walk around the house for a few days with a blocked nose calling your mum 'Bum' instead of Mum and saying things like, 'Heddo bum, dib you sleep well?' But when your mouth is stuck together and your nose is blocked you tend to find yourself in a rather serious situation which could actually kill you. Why? Because no air can get in and no air can get out! And when you have no air, you have no oxygen and you need oxygen to give your body energy to pump your heart and spread the blood through your limbs and organs and make your body work. So without oxygen your body just stops working and slowly starts to fall into a very deep sleep. And that's what was happening to Mum!

'Hey,' said the tongue from deep inside the closed chasm that was Mum's mouth. 'Is anyone starting to feel really tired and weak and sort of just wanting to go to sleep?'

'Yeah me,' said the toenails.

'Me too,' said the knuckles.

'MMMMMMMme too,' said Eppie. 'I

just want to sleep and sleep and sleep and sleep and dream that I'm married to gorgeous Prince William and he adores me and we make blockbuster movies together and I look just like Posh Spice.'

'You don't look anything like Posh Spice,' yawned Zeke. 'You look more like her pet poodle.'

'Thank you, Zeke,' said Eppie, 'but I couldn't care less because I haven't got the energy to argue and I really just want to be very still and very, very quiet.'

'Yeah, be quiet,' said the neck. 'I'm getting tired too.'

'Oh be quiet Neck,' said the feet. 'We're all getting tired.'

'Sssssssssssssssssssssh,' said the dimples in Mum's cheeks.

'Shhhhhhh, shhhhhhhh, shhhhhhh,' said every single incey wincey bincey sincey bit of Mum's body. 'Shhhhh, shhhhhhh, shhhhh,' they said, making a cacophony of sound until Brain roared,

'**Be quiet,** I'm tired and I've got a headache!'

'Uh oh,' whispered everything and then went suddenly silent.

Shhhhhhhhhhhhhhhhhh

Meanwhile, in the surgery, the doctor was beginning to panic. 'Oh no, oh no, oh no!' he squealed like a mad, mad mouse. 'This poor woman can't get any air! If we don't do something soon her body will fall asleep and then she won't know to try and breathe and so she will surely die! Quick!' he called to Nurse Whoppergob who was eating fourteen cream buns in the kitchen. 'Come here quickly. This woman's mouth is shut tight–tight. We must clear her nose immediately so that she can breathe.'

'Oh OK,' mumbled Nurse Whoppergob. 'But what will we use to clear her nose? A fire extinguisher, a vacuum cleaner or a straw?'

'Could you remind me to sack you when this drama is over?' said the doctor. 'And until then, let's try to clear this mother's nose with a traditional hanky.'

'OK,' grumbled Nurse Whoppergob as she shoved a whole bunch of tissues up to Mum's nose and bellowed like a trumpet, **'BLOW!'**

Well, Mum tried to blow but she couldn't. She quite simply couldn't. She couldn't get air through either nostril because her nostrils were clogged with thick gooey cold–muck (oh yuk) and no amount of nose blowing would shift it.

'OK,' said the doctor after Mum had tried four hundred and seventeen goes at blowing. 'That's not going to work. Let's tip this mother upside down. If her nose can't blow away all the snotty goop then the snotty goop will just have to run out.'

'I can't lift her up and turn her upside down,' said Nurse Whoppergob. 'I've just finished eating fourteen cream buns and I'm feeling very tired myself.'

'Well you couldn't be as tired as me,' said the doctor. 'I've been playing exhausting golf all morning. And last night I had to take my yacht for a race all round the harbour while entertaining the King of Balolo. So I'm far, far, far, far, far too drained to lift this grown woman and tip her upside down.'

'Well I don't see why she can't tip herself upside down,' said Nurse

Whoppergob, while she licked the cream bun crumbs from her hands and nearly ate her own fingers. 'I mean it is her nose after all!'

'Good idea,' said the doctor. 'We'll get her to tip herself upside down and then we'll give her the bill.'

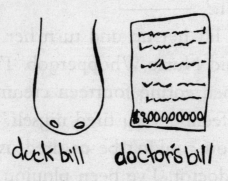

duck bill   doctor's bill

'Excuse me Madam,' the doctor said very loudly to Zeke and Eppie's mum who was now feeling very, very drowsy. 'Excuse me Madam, but if you don't mind we would like you to stand on your head please.'

'Mm?' said Mum.

'IMMEDIATELY!' said the doctor.

'Mmmmmmmmmmmmmmmmmmmmmm
mmmmmmmmmmmmmmmmmmmmm,' said
Mum, which means 'Ooooooooooooooo
ooooooooooooooooooooooooooh OK.'

And then Mum tried to
stand on her head.

For a brief moment Zeke
and Eppie's mother was
actually successful, but just
as her upside-down skirt
was about to flop over
her head and show the
whole world the enormous
underpants she was wearing, Mum
suddenly somersaulted onto the floor and
rolled right out the door.

'Whooooooaaaaa,'
screamed all the bits and pieces of Mum's
body as they were woken from their
sleepiness and rolled round and round and
upside down like a big dipper at the fair.

'Whooooooooo oooooooooooooaaa aaaaaa,' yelled Zeke and Eppie as they rumbled and tumbled around and around.

It probably would have been all right if Mum had just rolled out to the garden and stopped right there – so long as a dog didn't lift its leg on her. But Mum didn't just roll out the door and stop in the garden, she rolled down the driveway and past the front gate and out onto the footpath. Down she rolled past the prickly roses next door and the bus stop and a very crowded bus. Down past the park and the post office and the shops she went, going faster and faster and faster. Then she came to a hill and she rolled even more, like a tennis ball careering down a mountain, or a two-legged leopard wearing roller blades. Faster and faster and faster she rolled, past the school and the kids who were in the playground at recess.

'Hey, wasn't that Zeke and Eppie's mum?' said Claire Blump, the teacher's pet.

'Yes, um, ah, I think it was,' slurped goody-two-shoes Darryn Pinky.

'Well I'm sure she doesn't have a licence to roll down the road like that,' said Claire Blump.

'No,' said Darryn, 'I really think we

must report her.' And so off they went to snitch on Zeke and Eppie's mum. And Mum just kept rolling uncontrollably down the hill towards the highway.

She rolled into the gutter, she rolled onto the road, she rolled straight through the intersection, and turned right into Belbot Street, WITHOUT EVEN INDICATING! And then she went onto the highway.

She rolled under a truck and under another truck and under an even bigger truck and under an even bigger, bigger, bigger truck and accidentally caught a lift under a truck that was carrying twenty-four skunks to the zoo.

'Oh pong, what's that smell?' said Stinker the small skunk.

'It's a human,' said Stinker's mother.

And then when the truck stopped at the lights Mum rolled out from between

the wheels and rolled off the highway,
past small towns, past big farms, past
kangaroos and wombats and lots of
platypuses until she stopped with a
gigantic bumperoony when she hit a
very large crocodile, bounced off its nose
and landed in an emu's nest, where she
lay curled up in a ball and was sat on
by Ermantine the emu who thought she
was an egg.

mum

eggs

The bad thing about landing in an
emu's nest is that you get an emu's bum
on your head. But the good thing about
it is that when Mum hit the croc she

bumped with such a sudden thump that
little Zeke and Eppie were knocked loose
from between Mum's teeth and tumbled
safely under their mum's tongue.

'Yippeeee,' said Zeke.

'Yippeeee,' said Eppie.

'Uh oh,' said the pulse.

'Pulse, you're such a party pooper,'
said Tummy Button. 'What did you say
uh oh for?'

'I said uh oh,' replied Pulse sadly,
'because I think the crocodile bump has
knocked Mum unconscious.'

And sure enough, Mum had stopped
moving. She wasn't rolling any more
and she certainly wasn't mmmmmmmm
mmmmmmmmmmmmmmmmmmumbling.

Something very bad had happened and all of Mum's body could feel it in Mum's bones.

'Hey Eyes! What's happened?' asked the knuckles. 'Tell us what's happening.'

'We don't know,' said the eyes. 'We're closed.'

'Well for heaventh' thake, can't you open up and thee?' said the hips, who had a lisp.

'No we can't open up,' said the eyes as enormous tears welled in their corners and they began to cry. 'We need Brain's permission and he's not responding to our messages.'

'Did you send the messages through the nerves? I mean, are you sure that the messages got through?' asked the tiny hairs on Mum's arms. 'Because those nervous nerves get so confused when they're stressed that they really can't be trusted.'

'Oh no,' said Mum's veins. 'If we can't get messages to the brain we're definitely all going to die.'

'OH HOW TRAGIC,' said the heart in a very deep solemn voice.

'We really have got a terrible problem here,' said the wisdom teeth, 'and we need to fix it. The lack of oxygen has affected Brain and if he breaks down then we all do. We are now obviously in a race against time to travel up to the brain and fix the problem.'

'Oh no, oh no, oh no,' said the trembling nerves.

'I know a good mechanic who might be able to help,' said the left foot. 'She fixed the brake pedal in Mum's car, no worries.'

'Would you really want a grubby mechanic with a wrench fiddling around with our brain?' said the neck.

'Well what about the man who comes

to clean the house?' suggested the lips.
'He fixed the vacuum cleaner and he's
very nice and very good-looking.'

'Oh for heaven's sake, Lips,' said the
wrists. 'Don't you ever stop thinking
about kissing! We need someone to take
a good look at Brain, not someone who
is good-looking!'

'The only way to know what's going
on,' said the mole on Mum's shoulder,
'is if one of us can get up to Brain and
look around. But that adventurer will
have to cross blood rapids, mountains of
muscle and valleys of um . . . ah . . . do
you think Mum's listening? No, well
um, fat. That adventurer will have to
cross wild terrain that has never been
crossed, climb the unmapped territory of
Mum's body and then mend her brain.'

'Well we're not going,' said the ankles.
'We want to relax and put our feet up.'

'Well good,' said the eyelids. 'Because

we need an adventurer who is stronger than steel, braver than a lion and small as a ladybird.'

‘I'll go,’ said Tummy Button heroically.

‘Don't be ridiculous,' said everybody else.

‘We need Rambo,' said Skin.

‘We need Tarzan,' said the earlobes.

‘We need Superman and Wonderwoman!' said the eyebrows.

‘Yeah, that's who we need!' chorused the tastebuds. ‘We need Superman and Wonderwoman.'

‘But where are we going to find heroes like that?' said the lashes. ‘It's not like they're going to be just walking by!'

‘Oh sigh,' said the thighs.

‘We could put an ad in the Superhero Herald,' said the left shoulder.

‘Oh who's going to pay for that?'

scoffed the left collarbone nastily.

'Don't fight,' said the tummy. 'I can't stomach it right now. What we need is a brain to think of a solution.'

'I have a brain,' said Eppie.

'No you don't,' said Zeke.

'Be quiet,' said Eppie. 'I'm going to save Mum's life. If you want to come with me then you're welcome, but for once in our lives there's something more important than our fighting.'

'OK Eppie,' said Zeke. 'I'm very sorry, you're absolutely right. Whether you have a brain or not is not really the issue. Nor is it important that when you wake up you look like a pair of old underpants that have been worn by a donkey. No, what is important is that we rescue Mum right here and now. Come on Eppie, follow me!'

'No,' said Eppie, 'you follow me.'

'No, you follow me,' said Zeke.

'No you follow me.'

'No you follow me.'

'You will both follow me,' said a soft sweet voice that interrupted Zeke and Eppie.

'Who are you?' said Mum's muscles as they flexed themselves until they became enormous . . . well, the size of a peanut at least.

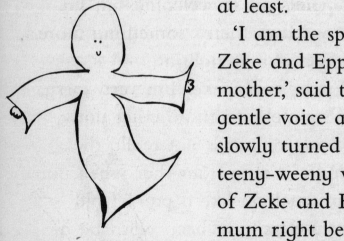

'I am the spirit of Zeke and Eppie's mother,' said the gentle voice as she slowly turned into a teeny-weeny version of Zeke and Eppie's mum right before their eyes. 'And I have come to look after Zeke and Eppie while they make their journey through their mother's body and up into her brain.'

'Oh isn't that sweet,' said the heart.

'And I have also come to make sure they stop fighting and are very polite to everyone they meet along the way. Normally I would also make sure that they had tidied their rooms, eaten their breakfasts and cleaned their teeth, but in this particular case, seeing as they are locked inside their mother's mouth, those last few points are irrelevant. Now, let's hurry up because I have in my hand your mother's internal clock, and it says we only have a matter of minutes before your mother's entire body shuts down.'

'Tic-tic-tic,' went Mum's internal clock.

'Ah, excuse me,' said Eppie.

'Yes,' said the spirit of their mother.

'Well, Spirit of Mother is quite a difficult name to call

in a hurry,' said Eppie. 'And I was wondering if you had a nickname we could call you?'

'Why yes,' said the spirit of Zeke and Eppie's mother. 'My nickname is Funky Chick.'

'I think I'd rather call you Spirit of Zeke and Eppie's mum,' said Zeke.

'Well I think I'll call you Mini-mum,' said Eppie. 'Me too,' Zeke agreed.

'OK, that's settled then. Time to go,' said Mini-mum. 'And if you two manage to stop fighting until the end of our journey I'll buy you both a vegetable ice cream.'

'Gross,' said Eppie.

'I don't like vegetables,' said Zeke.

'All right, I'll buy you some crisps,' said Mini-mum. 'But you'll have to share a packet.'

And so for the first time since they were born Eppie and Zeke stopped fighting. And for the first time they both heard silence. Which sounded exactly like this,

(shhhhhhh)

And then the silence was gently filled with the beating of Mum's slowing heart, the pulsing of Mum's slowing veins and the enormous throaty roar of Mini-mum yelling,

'Hurry up or we'll be late. Let's get a wriggle on!'

And with that Zeke and Eppie swung from Mum's tonsils and dived down her throat.

'Goodbye! Good luck!' cried all their new-found friends as Zeke and Eppie leapt into their adventure, plummeting out of control until they landed,

PLOP SQUIRT PLOP SPLAT!

After a moment Zeke and Eppie opened their shocked eyes and realised they were in their mother's stomach and it was filled with chocolate bars and lollies.

mum's tum

'Oh my gosh, get a load of this!' said Zeke, pointing to the pile of treats that was sitting in the corner of their mum's tum.

'Hey, look, this chocolate bar isn't even opened!' squealed Eppie delightedly as she ripped the wrapper and began to gobble down the chocolate as fast as she could so that the spirit of their mother wouldn't bust her.

'Are you all right over there Eppie?' called Mini-mum over her shoulder as she continued to look for signs pointing the way to Mum's brain.

'Yush,' said Eppie with a very full mouth. 'I'm abtholytely schwell.'

'Oh really Eppie?' said Mini-mum. 'I thought you might be scoffing a chocolate bar. And what about you, Zeke? I have a sneaking suspicion you're stuffing your face with a party-size bag of lollies?'

'How did she know that?' Zeke whispered to Eppie as he stuffed his face with a party-size bag of lollies. 'She must have eyes in the back of her head like mum.'

'Whatever you do, don't gobble,' said Mini-mum, 'or you'll disturb your mother's tummy and you'll never know what might happen.'

Suddenly there was a grumbling rumbling.

'Oh no,' said Mini-mum,

'Hang on for your life!'

'Oh yeah, good idea,' said Zeke. 'You're stuck in your mother's stomach with nothing but your mother's spirit, lots of junk food and your stinky sister and you're told to hang on for your life! Hang on to what dare I ask? A piece of rubbish food or your sister? Mmmmmmm hard to tell the difference.'

'RRRRRRRRRRR

RRRRRRRRRUmble.
GRRRRRRRRRRRR
RRRRRRRRRUmble.'

'Hang on to each other!' called Mini-mum as she came running towards them in that funny sort of fast-walk way that mothers do when they're wearing high heels and carrying a handbag and trying not to mess up their hair. 'And for heaven's sake stop guffling your gobs with all of those sweets and chocolates!'

But it was too late, Mum's rrrrrrrrrrrrrrrrrrrrrrrrrrrrrrrrrrrrrrrrrrrrumbles and grrrrrrrrrrrrrrrrrrrrrrrrrrrrrrrrrrrrrrumbles had turned into BURPS. And before you know it, Zeke and Eppie were suddenly wrapped in a wind tunnel of air and sent gaburping through their mother's stomach and back up her throat as well.

Whoosh gaburble they hurtled out
Mum's throat. And they would have
been fired like cannonballs straight out
Mum's mouth, but of course Mum's
mouth was tightly shut, and so they
bashed into the roof of Mum's mouth
and whooshed all the way back into her
tummy again.

Grrrrrrrrrrrrrrrrrrrrrrrrrrrrrrrrrrrrrrrrrrrrrr
rrrrrumble, rruuuuuuuuuuuuuuuumble.

'Look out!' cried Mini-mum. 'Here
comes another one!' And sure enough, no
sooner had Zeke and Eppie returned to

Mum's stomach than they were sent gaburbling back out again. Again and again and again it happened because their mother was like a burping machine!

'When is this ever going to stop?' called Eppie as she whooshed off and bashed into the inside of Mum's closed mouth again.

'When you two stop disturbing your mum's stomach by doing all that chewing,' said Mini-mum.

'Gulp,' said Zeke and Eppie and the burping stopped.

'Now,' said Mini-mum after Zeke and Eppie had landed thump back in the stomach again. 'I want both of you to settle down. The one good thing about all that burping is that it may have given your mother a bit of extra air and therefore given us more time to get to Brain and rescue her. Now, I'll just check the clock.'

'Yes, I was right,' continued Mini-mum, 'we have two and a half minutes in out-of-body time which is about seven and a half minutes in here. Excellent. That should give us just long enough, so long as nothing goes wrong. Now tidy your hair and straighten your clothes, stand up straight and get those sulky looks off your faces. There's plenty of time to eat chocolate and lollies when you're as old as your mother. OK then team, off we go. We have a mission to accomplish.'

Somehow, from somewhere, loud music began to play. Very loud exciting hero music like something from a Star Wars movie. *Da da da da da da*. It made Zeke feel very strong and proud but it made Eppie want to do something else. All of a sudden she began to shake and tremble, lift her legs and her arms up in the air and give her bottom a wriggle.

back view of Eppie dancing

'What on earth are you doing?' asked Zeke and Mini-mum.

'I'm dancing of course,' said Eppie.

'Dancing! You absolutely must be joking,' said Zeke. 'At a time like this!'

'It's not my fault,' said Eppie angrily. 'You know I have an allergic reaction to music and it just makes me want to dance. It's not my fault the music came on.'

'Oh that's your mother's internal stereo,' said Mini-mum. 'Your mother has it on nearly all the time . . . you know how she sings and hums. Well, I'd hoped that it would inspire you if I let it play but it never occurred to me that it would turn Eppie into a mad dancing ceiling fan. I think we'll stop the music immediately.' But Mini-mum needn't have worried, because the music suddenly stopped with a terrible *sceeeeeeeeeeeeeeeeeeeeeeech*.

'Oh no, this is a very bad sign!' said Mini-mum. 'The energy that was needed to run Mum's internal stereo isn't strong enough now to keep it going. She's fading away. Quick, quick we really must hurry. Now do up your shoes and let's run to the brain.'

And so Zeke and Eppie ran with their mother's spirit to the very end of their mother's stomach, leaping over packets of chips and chocolate bars and the occasional glass of white wine.

But when they came to an intersection with several different paths Zeke and Eppie were all huffed and puffed and didn't have a clue which way to go.

'Oh dear,' said Mini-mum as she floated beside Zeke and Eppie, 'this is a disaster. We were going to catch a lift with the blood flow because normally you know where the blood's flowing, what time it will be departing, what time it will arrive, first stop here, second stop there, you know, kidneys, appendix, small intestine. But now that Mum's system is breaking down all the roads are changing.'

'Oh boo hoo boo hoo,' said Eppie. 'What shall we do, do, do, do, do?'

'I know, we'll go to the liver. She'll help us sort out what information we need and then we'll move on from there,' said Mini-mum.

And so the three of them ran along the squishy path that said TO THE LIVER with their feet slurping and fulurping through the gooey slick. When they finally arrived at the liver they found she wasn't feeling too good herself.

'Hello Liver,' said Mini-mum. 'My, you're looking a bit pale.'

'Yes,' said the liver. 'I just don't seem to have any idea what's wrong with me today. I feel weak and tired and unable to work. In fact I just want to snooze.'

'No, don't snooze,' said Eppie. 'We need your help.'

But the liver had started to snooze and snore. 'Hugh, hoogh, hugh, hugh, hugh, hugh.'

'WAKE UP!'
blustered Mini-mum desperately in a voice that woke Mum's entire body. (In fact, all over the world children and Dads probably heard that bellow and automatically got out of bed and started to get ready for school or work or uni.)

Oh yes indeedy, when you hear that sort of voice you don't argue with it, you just do whatever it says. If that voice had roared *stick your fingers up your nose* the whole world probably would have. So it's just lucky that the voice only said, 'Wake up'. And that's exactly what the liver did.

'We need to know which way to go to get up to Brain,' said Zeke. 'Can you help us please?'

'Well many of the roads are cut off today,' said Liver. 'But what I suggest is you ignore all side streets, back lanes and detours and just get on one of the main arteries and follow the signs as you go.' Then the liver fell back to sleep and Zeke began to sob, although he tried to hide it by pretending he had a frog stuck in his throat.

'Crebbit, crebbit, crebbit,' spluttered Zeke.

'Hold my hands,' said Mini-mum, 'I will look after you.' And so Zeke and Eppie held the spirit of their mother's hands while she covered them in a thick gooey sticky love that formed a protective bubble around them. Then, before you know it, Zeke and Eppie and Mini-mum were in a love bubble and bouncing up the road to the main artery.

For a short time the three of them were delighted. They were sure they had found the short cut to Mum's brain and would have her fixed up in a matter of moments. But after a while the artery began to get cluttered with strange objects with very frightening faces and they were bashing against the bubble.

'Aaaaaaaaaaaaaaaaaaaaaaaaaaaaaaaaa aaaaaaaaaaaaagh,' screamed Zeke as he saw one up close, 'those things look just like you Eppie!'

'What are they?' asked Eppie.

'They're germs,' Mini-mum replied, trying to stay calm. 'They must have heard that your mother is getting weak and they've begun an invasion.'

'But we have to fight them!' said Zeke.

'How?' wailed Eppie. 'There are so many of them.'

'Well we'll have to fight them with something that makes things drop dead,' said Mini-mum.

'I suppose I could try my dancing,' said Eppie. 'Those man-o'-war guards died of embarrassment in our last adventure when they saw me shakin' my booty.' And with that Eppie started to do her famous 'cockroach lying on his back' dance, but she was so sad and so tired that she just looked like an early flying machine that couldn't take off into the sky. So the germs just ignored her and more began to appear.

'I'm sorry,' Eppie said sadly. 'It just didn't work.'

'Here, let me have a go,' said Mini-mum. 'I'll try bossing them away.' And so she yelled at the top of her voice, 'How dare you be such bullies? If you don't stop I'm going to tell your mothers, your school, the police and SANTA!'

But the germs only laughed in their wicked cruel way 'ha ha hi hi hoo hoo.' Then all of a sudden the alarm on Mum's internal clock rang.

DDDDDDDDDD DDDDring.

'Oh no!' said Mini-mum. 'That means we've got just two minutes left.'

'Zeke, you try something,' said Eppie. 'You're good at killing things.'

'What!' exclaimed Zeke.

'You are,' said Eppie. 'I've seen you kill flies, ants, mosquitoes and snails.'

'All right, I'll try something,' said Zeke. 'But I haven't got a magnifying glass here with me, and these germs don't have wings.'

'Well why don't you try telling one of your terrible jokes?' said Eppie. 'They're so bad, they kill me every time.'

'Well thank you for that,' said Zeke, a little irritated. 'But all right, for the sake of our mum I will try. Hey germs,' he said very loudly so the germs could hear him through the bubble, 'hey guys, how do monsters like their eggs? Terrifried!'

A few germs moaned and a few germs groaned but none actually seemed to die.

'Try another joke,' said Eppie. 'What about the one about the rabbit.'

'Oh yeh,' said Zeke. 'That one's a killer. Hey germs! What do you call a rabbit with fleas? Bugs Bunny!'

'Boo boo boo,' said the germs and one hundred and seven died.

'Good,' said Mini-mum. 'One hundred and seven germs dead and only four hundred and eighty-three billion to go. You're definitely making them weaker. Have you got any more jokes up your sleeve Zeke?'

'Yes,' said Zeke. 'I have one that will slay this crowd. Hey germs, why did the tomato stop in the middle of the road? Because he wanted to play SQUASH!'

The air was filled with agonised squawks and cries of 'Oh! Ouch! That joke was so bad.' And within milli-seconds, after twisting and writhing, all the germs dropped dead . . . except for one, which quietly pierced the bubble and stung Eppie on the arm and Zeke on the leg.

'All right then,' said Mini-mum. 'We have one and a half minutes to get to Brain.' But Zeke and Eppie were starting to feel so sick that they simply couldn't move.

'What's the matter?' the spirit of their mother asked kindly.

'A germ got us,' said Eppie.

'We feel sick,' said Zeke.

'Oh no! Not at a time like this!' said Mini-mum. 'Oh dear, what can we do?'

'I know, I'll take you to your mother's heart, perhaps that will make you better.'

bright idea

'But how can we have time when we have to rush to the brain?' asked Eppie.

'A visit to your mum's heart will not only strengthen you but it will strengthen your mum as well. It will remind her of all that is wonderful in her life and give us more precious seconds to fix her up again.'

'Oh OK,' said Zeke and Eppie with their shoulders stooped and their eyes filled with tears.

After just a few moments they arrived at Mum's heart and although Heart was getting tired she was filled with a red-golden light. As soon as Zeke and Eppie walked inside Heart they began to laugh and giggle.

Mum's heart was filled
with a thousand drawers
and doors and behind
each one was a special
memory of the times the
three of them had shared.

There were the times when Zeke and
Eppie were born, the time that Zeke
vomited on Grandma, and the time
baby Eppie pooed on Pop. There were
all the times they'd cooked dinner
together, all the times they'd danced in
the living room, all the time Eppie had
made up plays and all the time Zeke
had made Mum play football with him
inside the house. There were snuggly
times in bed on a Saturday morning and
grumpy times when no one would go to
sleep, there were happy times like when
Mum won the school sack race and sad
times like when their puppy got run
over. Every chamber of Mum's heart

contained different thoughts and memories and as Zeke and Eppie wandered through they were filled with such love and happiness that they knew they had the strength to do anything.

'Are you ready to go now?' asked Mini-mum very gently.

'Yes,' said Zeke and Eppie at last like Superman and Wonderwoman. 'Of course we are!'

And so they returned to their bubble and flowed with the artery's current upwards towards the brain.

Meanwhile, back in the desert, where Ermantine the emu was sitting on a strange Mum-egg, Mum was beginning to feel warm stirrings in her heart as she was filled with the love of Zeke and Eppie. And those warm stirrings made her wriggle with happiness even though she had a bird's bum on her head.

mum is under here

Wriggle, wriggle, wriggle, went Mum in the nest.

Tickle, tickle, tickle, felt Ermantine on her bottom.

Wriggle, wriggle, wriggle, went Mum in the nest.

Giggle, giggle, giggle, went Ermantine.

Wriggle, wriggle, wriggle, went Mum in the nest.

Guffaw, guffaw, guffaw, went
Ermantine so loudly and hysterically that
the local handsome park ranger whose
truck had broken down just up the road
came over to investigate.

'Oh, Ermantine, it's you,' said Perfect
Pete the Park Ranger. 'Why are you
making that shocking sound?'

'Oh, Perfect Pete,' said Ermantine as
she batted her eyelids and preened her
feathers and tried to
look incredibly
beautiful. 'I'm a little
embarrassed to say, but
the very large egg in
my nest seems to be
tickling my bottom.'

'Here, let me take a
look,' said Perfect Pete
the Park Ranger.

Perfect Pete

'At my bottom?' said Ermantine.

'No, at the egg,' said Perfect Pete.

'Oh,' mumbled Ermantine as she rose from her nest and Perfect Pete found Zeke and Eppie's mum curled up in a tight little ball with a whopper bump on her head.

'Oh, my goodness, it's a woman and she's very very ill!' exclaimed Perfect Pete. 'We must get her to a doctor straight away. But wait, my truck has broken down...Oh beautiful Ermantine, will you give us a ride to the local hospital please?'

'What did you say?' said Ermantine.

'I asked if you would take us to the local hospital, pleeeeeeeeease,' said Perfect Pete the Park Ranger.

'No,' said Ermantine, 'the bit about me being beautiful.'

'I said, oh beautiful Ermantine will you give us a ride to the local hospital,' repeated the Park Ranger.

'Why certainly, handsome,' said Ermantine.

And so Perfect Pete, who looked like Leonardo Di Caprio, except with much bigger muscles, lifted Mum onto Ermantine's back and then hopped on behind her. Then they rode as fast as they could through the desert until they came to a small tin shed.

'Here we are,' said Ermantine. 'This is the hospital.'

'Thanks,' said Perfect Pete.

'How about a date to go dancing on Saturday night?' said Ermantine.

'I'm sorry, I can't go on a date,' said Perfect Pete. 'I'm married.'

'Damn,' said Ermantine as she ran off.

'Damn,' said Mum in her sleep.

damn

'Oh doctor, oh doctor,' called Perfect Pete as he knocked on the tiny hospital door. But the doctor was out visiting a patient who had foolishly stuck a peanut up his nose and now had peanut trees growing out of his ears.

Quickly Perfect Pete checked to see how much longer Zeke and Eppie's mum had to live. 'Oh no,' groaned Perfect Pete as he checked her pulse. 'It seems to me this lovely creature,' (Mum wrote that bit) 'has passed away already. Oh what a waste of such a magnificent woman,' (Mum wrote that bit too). And so he began to sob.

Meanwhile Zeke and Eppie and Mini-mum had made it to the top of Mum's head and what they saw was no big disaster, just a wilting brain that needed oxygen, like plants need regular watering. So quickly they ran all around Mum's brain and opened every window they could find. And sure enough, the air did flow through but not nearly strongly enough.

'We need a really big blast of air,' wheezed the lungs, who had been woken from their sleep by the flowing breeze.

'But how will we get a big blast of air?' asked the blood cells.

'I know!' said the waking eyes. 'Look out there, at that handsome stranger, he can breathe into Mum's lungs by giving her the kiss of life.'

'But he's married,' said the finger next to Mum's thumb, the one she did all the pointing with. 'There's no way he's going to touch Mum's lips.'

'No, he's not married,' said the heart. 'He just said that because he doesn't like going dancing with Ermantine because she always treads on his toes and tells everyone he's her boyfriend.'

'All right,' said Mini-mum, who rather liked Perfect Pete herself. 'Let's all think about the park ranger kissing, sorry, I mean giving mouth-to-mouth resuscitation to Zeke and Eppie's mum and perhaps our thoughts will enter the park ranger's mind and he will do as we wish.' And so they all thought hard. The ankles thought, the ears thought and so did Mum's little pinkies. Every single part of Mum's body thought about a big moooshy kiss, sorry, I mean mouth-to-mouth resuscitation.

And it worked! Perfect Pete took a deep breath and breathed into Mum's lungs and she came back to life.

'YEAH!' cheered every part of Mum's body.

'YEAH!' cheered Mum.

'YEAH!' cheered Perfect Pete.

'YEAH!' cheered Zeke and Eppie. 'Now we can get out of Mum's body and finally all go home.'

Perfect Pete carried Mum over to the

hospital bed, even though, by this stage, she probably could have walked all by herself. And Mum let Perfect Pete tuck her in, and she let him make her a cup of tea, and she let him find her something to read.

'I'm afraid the magpies have stolen all the magazines,' said Perfect Pete, 'because they just love to catch up on all the gossip. So the only things you can possibly read here are a medical report I found at the front desk about someone whose head blew off in a storm, or else an old book that's full of all the different favourite children's stories.'

The Little Book of Favourite Children's Stories

'I'll read *The Little Book of Favourite Children's Stories*,' said Mum. 'It reminds me of something but I don't know what.'

Meanwhile Zeke and Eppie were sitting up in Mum's brain fiddling with all the files and wires trying to work out how on earth to get out again.

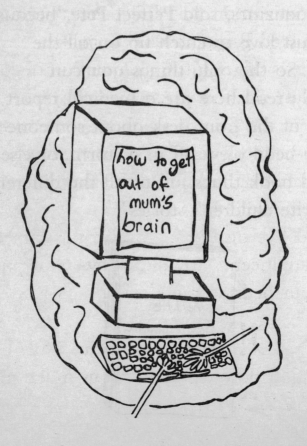

'Did you hear that?' said Zeke. 'Mum's sort of remembering we have that book at home. I wonder if she'll remember us when we get out of here!'

'If we ever do,' said Eppie softly.

'I've brought you a sandwich,' said Perfect Pete as he entered Mum's hospital room once more and found her reading 'Little Red Riding Hood' from the collection of favourite children's stories.

'Oh thanks, that's very nice of you,' said Mum, trying to sound like a woman who was really smart, interesting, funny and attractive but not in the least bit threatening.

'And I've also brought you this bunch of magnificent Fuzzyfluff flowers to put on your bedside table.'

'NO!' screamed Mum. 'Not Fuzzyfluff flowers, they always make me sneeze.'

'Oh I'm very sorry,' said Perfect Pete politely. 'I'll take them back out again.' But it was too late because the sneeze had started; it was tingling in Mum's toes and fidgeting in Mum's fingers and numbing Mum's nose and bubbling Mum's brain and focusing every single bit of Mum on the most enormous sneeze the world had ever seen.

'**Aaaah,** duck for cover!' yelled Mum.

And so Perfect Pete dived under Mum's bed while she **achooed** the most enormous sneeze that not only splattered goop all over *The Little Book of Favourite Children's Stories* but shot Zeke and Eppie straight out Mum's nose inside a ball of snot.

'Yippee,' said Zeke and Eppie as they flew through the air. 'Finally we're out!'

But they spoke too soon because the force of Mum's sneeze had not only hurtled them on to *The Little Book of Favourite Children's Stories* but it had forced them right into the pages of the story that Mum was reading at the time!

'Hello,' said the Big Bad Wolf to Zeke and Eppie. 'Now tell me, what have we here?'

TO BE CONTINUED

About the author, Gretel Killeen;

Gretel Killeen started writing comedy by accident when she stood up to perform a very serious poem and everybody laughed.

From here she moved to writing and performing comedy in a variety of theatres and clubs across her home country, Australia, and for a number of major radio stations. Gretel's comedy writing then led to television and in 2001 Gretel hosted Australia's *Big Brother* – a phenomenal success which she repeated in 2002.

Gretel has published a number of best-selling books that will split your sides and make your head explode. After you read them, you'll never be the same again.

She lives in Sydney's famous Bondi with her two children, Zeke and Eppie – the stars and illustrators of the *My Sister's a Yo-yo*, *My Sister's an Alien*, *My Sister's a Burp* and *My Sister's a Sea Slug*.

GRETEL KILLEEN

My Sister's a YO-YO

When Eppie falls into a pothole, gets **squashed** to the size of a **strawberry** and becomes completely **entangled** in her brother Zeke's **yo-yo**, Zeke only has a day to get her back to normal. What follows is a **hilarious** high tale of **escape**, theft, bullies, **brats**, goody-goodies, garbage trucks, **magic** lamps, **scabs**, snot, bribery, **bravery**, a blind mum, a fat nurse, a **skinny teacher** and a boy on a bicycle covered in something **very unsavoury** – and that's only the beginning!

'Short–every–second inventive fun'
JACQUELINE WILSON

0099433680
£3.99

GRETEL KILLEEN

My Sister's an
Alien

When Eppie gets **squished** to the size of a strawberry, ends up **flying** round the world, landing on planet sock and about to be kidnapped by a **handsome alien** prince, it's up to her brother Zeke to rescue her. What follows is a **laugh-a-minute** adventure full of short-sighted cats, space rockets, **burps**, possums, owls, **goodies**, **baddies**, galactic battles, **movie stars**, superstars, false **moustaches**, girls' nighties, flying horses, footballs, diamonds, **lovesick Martians** and motorbike rides with the man in the moon – and that's all before Mum wakes up.

'Madly inventive and very funny'
JACQUELINE WILSON

0099433672

£3.99

GRETEL KILLEEN

My Sister's a Sea Slug

When Eppie and Zeke get **stretched** like spaghetti it's only a matter of time before they are **sucked** down the plughole and into a new adventure. What follows is a **giggle-filled** non-stop underwater **romp**, with man-eating seaweed, pirates in petticoats, secret castles, **magic mermaids**, fat fisherman, **splendid** speedy sea cycles, **elastic** eels, and **supersonic** horses . . . and that's all before breakfast!

0099448076

£3.99